DAVID LUCAS

LOST
in the
TOY
MUSEUM

—an adventure—

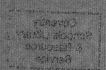

WALKER BOOKS
AND SUBSIDIARIES
LONDON · BOSTON · SYDNEY · AUCKLAND

When the lights went out at the Toy Museum
and the doors were locked,
all the toys *woke up*.
They bounced down off the shelves,
giddy and laughing
and squeaking with delight.

But Bunting, the old toy cat,
just rolled his eyes and sighed.
He brushed his whiskers,
he stretched,
and slowly, slowly,
he got down from the shelf...

"Please assemble for inspection,"
said Bunting, just as he did every night.

He called the register,
and then he counted all the toys ...
twice ... just to be sure no one was missing.

He made sure that they
did their exercises.

heads,
shoulders,
knees
and toes
(knees
and toes)

He made sure that none of them
were broken or coming apart
at the seams.

loose threads?
wobbly eye?
squeaky joints?
stuffing
coming out?

please
queue
here

And then he began to talk
about the history of the Museum
– just as he did every night.

1872

But *that* night was different.
That night all the toys just ran away.

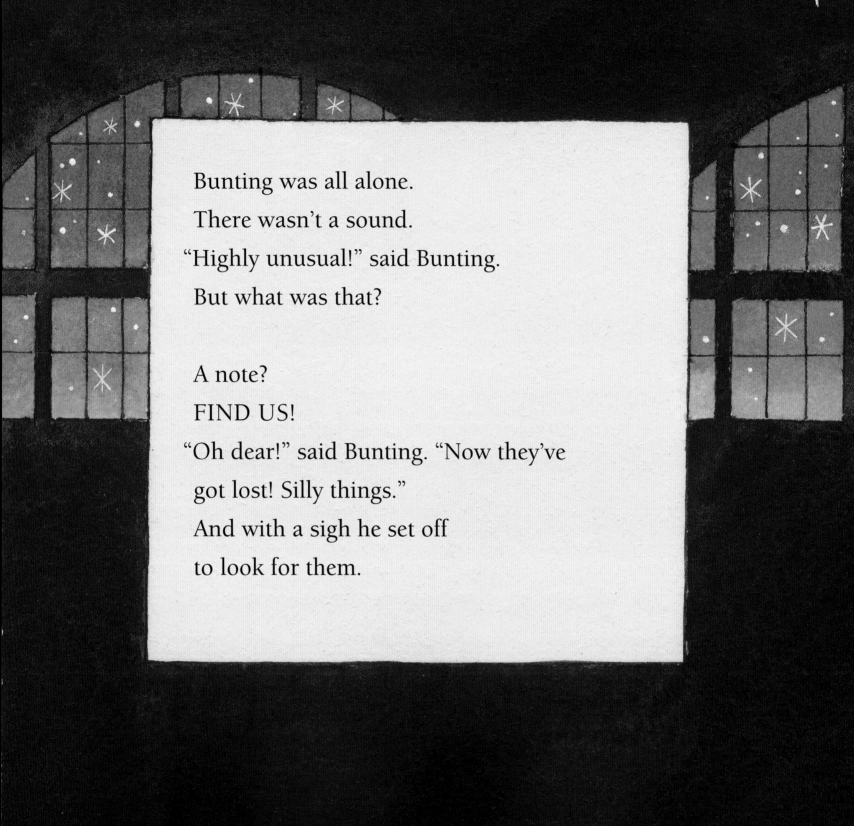

Bunting was all alone.
There wasn't a sound.
"Highly unusual!" said Bunting.
But what was that?

A note?
FIND US!
"Oh dear!" said Bunting. "Now they've
got lost! Silly things."
And with a sigh he set off
to look for them.

He looked for them everywhere.
They weren't in any of
the Dolls' Houses.

They weren't
in the Chinese Rock
Garden.

They weren't riding
on the Toy Railway.
Perhaps they were in the
Toy Theatre?
Bunting investigated.
There was a mysterious note:
GETTING WARMER.
But what did it *mean*?

He walked back through the scenery,
further than he'd ever dared go before.

And there was another note:
AND WARMER...
But what did it mean?

Then he heard
voices on the wind,
coming from across the sea.

He set sail.
He was alone on the water,
under the stars.
Now *he* was lost.
He didn't know *where*
he was at all.

But there was a message
in a bottle.
One word: COLDER.

Bunting turned
the boat around.
There, *at last*, was land!

And another note:
HOT! HOT! HOT!
(nearly on fire!!!).

"SURPRISE!"

all the toys leapt out of nowhere.

"Do you mean it's been a *game*, all along?"
  said Bunting.

"It *was* fun," they said, "wasn't it?"

"*Fun?*"

  Hmmm. Yes, he had to admit it *had* been fun.
  He'd been on an *adventure*.

"It's called *hide and seek*,"
  said the toys.

"Perhaps we could play it
  tomorrow night too?"
  said Bunting.

And now it was getting light.

But before they all hurried
back to the shelves
where they belonged,
Bunting called the register,
and counted them, *twice* ...
just to be sure.